Cottontail at Clover Crescent

SMITHSONIAN'S BACKYARD

To Margie Day Hamlin for whom rabbits dance—serendipity!—D.L.

I dedicate this book to those two paragons of patience and good humor, Dana and Lisa.—A.D.

Published by Soundprints, an imprint of Trudy Corporation, Norwalk, Connecticut.
www.soundprints.com

First Paperback Edition 2003
10 9 8 7 6 5 4 3
Printed in China

Acknowledgments:
Our very special thanks to the late Dr. Charles Handley of the Department of Vertebrate Zoology at the Smithsonian's National Museum of Natural History for his curatorial review.

ISBN 1-59249-112-X (pbk.)

The Library of Congress Cataloging-in-Publication Data below applies only to the hardcover edition of this book.

Library of Congress Cataloging-in-Publication Data

Lamm, C. Drew.

Cottontail at Clover Crescent / by C. Drew Lamm ; illustrated by Allen Davis.
p. cm.
Summary: A mother cottontail leaves her baby bunnies and goes looking for food while she listens to all the nighttime sounds around her, including the sounds of danger.
ISBN 1-59899-108-8
1, Cottontails — Juvenile fiction [1. Cottontails — Fiction. 2. Rabbits — Fiction.]
I. Davis, Allen, ill. II. Title.
PZ10.3.L33235Co 1995 94-28697
[E] — dc20 CIP
AC

Cottontail at Clover Crescent

by C. Drew Lamm

Illustrated by Allen Davis

It's a warm spring afternoon. The breeze is sweet with flowers. Cottontail rabbit sniffs the scented air behind the green house on Clover Crescent.

She gives birth to five bunnies in a nest in the lawn. It is her second litter this spring. And there will be more.

They do not look like rabbits—these squirming red creatures. These bald bunnies cannot hear or see. Their ears are smushed flat, and their eyes are squinched shut.

Before they were born, Cottontail gathered dried grass and pulled fur from her tummy to line their nest. It keeps them warm.

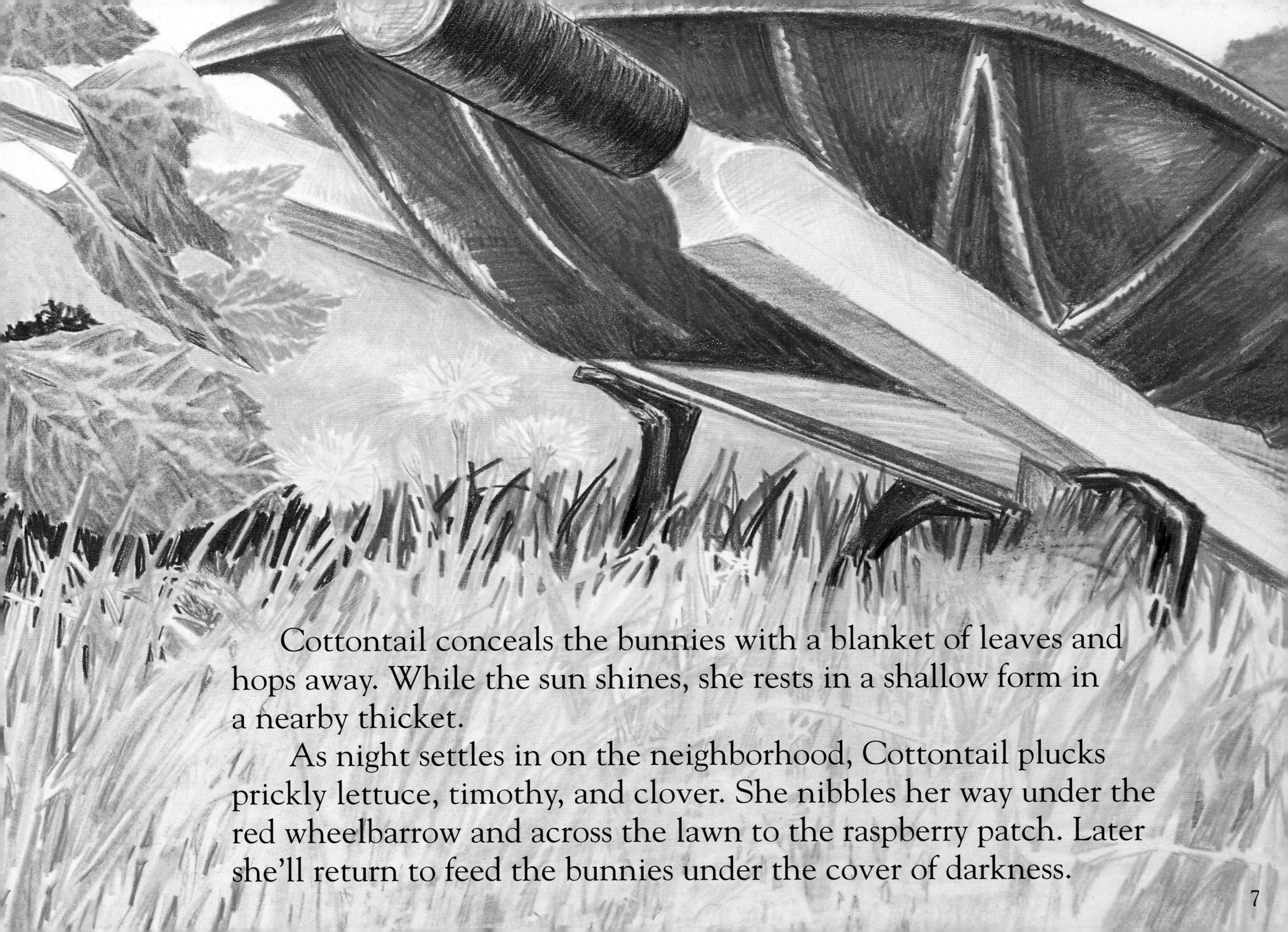

Cottontail conceals the bunnies with a blanket of leaves and hops away. While the sun shines, she rests in a shallow form in a nearby thicket.

As night settles in on the neighborhood, Cottontail plucks prickly lettuce, timothy, and clover. She nibbles her way under the red wheelbarrow and across the lawn to the raspberry patch. Later she'll return to feed the bunnies under the cover of darkness.

The moon rises just to the right of the chimney. A light in an upstairs bedroom clicks off. Only the moon lights the yard.

In a scramble of branches beside the raspberry patch, Cottontail licks her front paws. She drags her wet paws down over her face. Then she licks them again and drags them down her left ear—a long, soft ear that hears even the wind on one leaf.

While she cleans, she listens. A whippoorwill's whistle bursts into the air. She hears a baby opossum's sneeze. A skunk snuffles through the ground dining on grubs. Cottontail's ears swivel, alert to each rustle.

She ignores the wind in the leaves. She turns one ear at the sound of deer grazing beneath the trees. But at the beat of a wing, she freezes. The fur on the back of her neck bristles.

There are predators out at night. She fears the rush of a wing and the strike of a talon.

She scours the skies and spies a crow roosting high in the branches. She turns her head and loses sight of him. Unless he stirs again she won't see him among the dark branches. Her large eyes continue to search the darkness.

Leaves rustle high in the maple. Cottontail nibbles dandelion in the grass.

Wind brushes the grasses, bending them in dark waves. A shadow sweeps across the lawn.

Cottontail freezes. A blade of grass balances on her tongue. She feels the rush of a wing.

A barred owl plunges to the grass. It strikes a vole a few feet from Cottontail, and the vole is gone.

When the air stills, Cottontail twitches her nose. Slowly, she finishes chewing the blade of grass.

She sniffs the yard. The bunnies will be hungry. When she's certain it's safe, she returns to her nest.

Cottontail uncovers the bunnies. They stir and stretch. She crouches above them. They scramble over each other, their tiny mouths puckering. They reach up to drink their mother's sweet milk.

The smallest bunny, scrunched on the bottom, struggles hardest to get to the nourishment.

The bunnies finish suckling. Their bellies bulge, and their mouths are wet and milky. Drowsy and full—a nest of sleepy bunnies.

Cottontail covers them once more and hops away through the grass.

A full moon washes the white clover. Each flower shimmers. Cottontail quivers. Moonlight, warm night—she is poised to stretch.

Across the yard, a male cottontail lifts his head from a row of lettuce. Lettuce dangles under his wet nose. He crunches and pulls the large leaves in with each bite. They disappear into his pink mouth. He sits up.

Cottontail turns and crouches. As if music for a waltz has begun, Cottontail springs into the air.

She twirls and lands. And then she leaps again.

The male leaves the lettuce. Moonlight shines on his white tail puff. He tenses and leaps high into the air.

The rabbits twist and turn under the spring moon, peppering the dew with their paws. The clover Cottontail will munch by sunrise serves as a dance floor tonight.

Cottontails stretching. Cottontails leaping. Cottontails dancing.